TAE KWON DO
CLASH

BY JAKE MADDOX

Jake Maddox JV books are published by
Stone Arch Books
A Capstone imprint
1710 Roe Crest Drive
North Mankato, Minnesota 56003
www.mycapstone.com

Library of Congress Cataloging-in-Publication Data is available on the
Library of Congress website

ISBN: 978-1-4965-3981-6 (hardcover) 978-1-4965-3985-4 (paperback)
978-1-4965-3989-2 (ebook PDF)

Summary: Ben's mom tries to talk him into joining a rival tae kwon do studio, but Ben is
loyal to his instructor. If he could just get his nerves under control, the competition would
be his. Ben must work extra hard and use his instructor's somewhat eccentric techniques to
beat the rival studio's bully — as well as his nerves — at the national tournament.

Art Director: Nathan Gassman
Designer: Sarah Bennett
Production Specialist: Katy LaVigne

Photo Credits:
Shutterstock: Aaron Amat, design element, Brocreative, design element, Darkkong, cover,
DeanHarty, design element, hin255, design element, irin-k, design element, Kaderov Andrii,
design element

Printed and bound in the United States of America.
009622F16

TABLE OF CONTENTS

CHAPTER I

CHAMPIONSHIP JACKET

Ben bowed and stepped onto the training floor. He kicked at an imaginary opponent, warming up his muscles. He jacked up the power and made his pant legs snap.

After a few minutes, he put his feet together and bent over to stretch his hands to the floor. The slow burn felt fantastic. The tension in his hips and back released. The warmth flowing through his muscles passed along his lower back, down his legs, and out to his bare toes.

He slid into the splits and put his chest to the floor.

Mr. Ronson came out of the office. "You know," he said, looking at Ben, "they're hiring acrobats at the circus. You ought to apply."

Ben said, smiling, "This place is a circus."

"Some days it is," said Mr. Ronson. "Isn't it fun?" He smiled.

Tanner Hartke, Ben's best friend, stepped on the mat. "If this place is anything, it's definitely fun." Tanner tried to stretch as low as Ben and then started laughing as he fell over.

Mr. Ronson pointed at Ben. "This dude's like that guy in the Fantastic Four."

"Too bad he can't talk to a girl," said Tanner, getting up from his fall. "He gets so nervous he just walks away."

Ben got up, too, grinning at Tanner. Tanner grinned back, but then looked away, never meeting his eyes. Ben thought that was a little strange. Still,

Tanner was right — Ben got nervous really easily. Especially during tae kwon do competitions. In the last tournament, he'd gotten so nervous he almost messed up his chances of winning.

Mr. Ronson laughed and moved to the front of the class. He stood under the Korean flag, a tribute to tae kwon do's country of origin.

He said, "*Cha ryuht*," the Korean word for "attention," and "*choon bi*," the Korean word for "ready." He bowed to show respect to the students. The students bowed to show respect to him.

"As a sign of respect," Mr. Ronson said, "turn and bow to the parents." The parents in the sitting area stood up. The students turned and bowed to them. The parents bowed in return.

Mr. Ronson paced in front of the students. He said, "Class! Welcome. So, as you may know, we have awesomeness, right here among us." He stopped by a speaker in the corner of the room and his eyes twinkled. "So now, my friends, a magic trick." He reached down behind the speaker and pulled out a championship jacket. "The rewards of hard work!"

The back of the jacket said *National Tae Kwon Do Association Regional Champion Benjamin Davis.*

"Mr. Benjamin, sir," said Mr. Ronson, "step forward, please."

Ben said, "Yes, sir," and stepped forward. Mr. Ronson held up the jacket for Ben.

"The real magic," said Mr. Ronson, "was navigating the National Tae Kwon Do Association and their impossible levels of bureaucracy, but after waging a nonstop attack for about a year, I did get them to finally ship your jacket." Mr. Ronson draped the jacket over Ben's shoulders. "Now you can wear two jackets at a time. That'd be a good look for you — your normal jacket under your championship jacket. You'll start a new trend."

Students and parents snickered. Ben smiled.

"Mr. Benjamin," said Mr. Ronson. Ben loved how he always said "mister" before his first name. He'd called him "Mr. Benjamin" since he started at the *dojang*, even though Ben's last name was Davis. "What's your goal now? Win a couple of championships in the next tournament? Otherwise known as Districts?"

"Yes, sir," said Ben. "My goal is to win Districts."

"Yes," said Mr. Ronson, smiling, "we have a real slacker here." People giggled. "Do you realize, Mr. Benjamin, that last year you competed against thirteen- and fourteen-year-olds? This year, you must compete with fifteen-, sixteen-, and seventeen-year-olds. You, sir, will be but fifteen."

"Yes, sir."

"All right. Well, then, we'd better start training, Slacker," said Mr. Ronson with a wink. He looked at the whole class. "Line up and hit the bags."

Ben and his fellow tae kwon do students formed single-file lines in front of the two standing punching bags. The bags were a good 6 feet tall and filled with pounds and pounds of sand to keep them from getting knocked over.

Mr. Ronson said, "Think about *ki-haps*. If you engage an opponent with a good 'HI-YAH,' you could win the fight before it starts. Your concentration will be better. Your strikes more powerful. A good ki-hap helps you breathe. And we don't want anyone passing out from not breathing, right?" Students in the class smiled. "So give me some loud 'HI-YAH's."

The students yelled, "HI-YAH!" Ben thought he could hear his own yell echo around the room.

"Side kicks," said Mr. Ronson. "'HI-YAH!'"

Two by two, each of the twelve students attacked the bags, yelling, "HI-YAH!" The lines moved quickly as the students took their turns, and the yells filled up the entire room.

Ben watched as Tanner side kicked a bag and yelled, "HI-YAH!" It almost toppled over and Tanner grinned as he ran back in line. Ben low fived him when he took his place behind him. But for some reason, Tanner again didn't meet his eyes.

"Focus on breathing," said Mr. Ronson. "When you kick, exhale. 'HI-YAH!' If you can master your ki-haps, you can master your entire endocrine system."

Ben raised his hand. Still a little out of breath, he asked, "Sir, what is an endocrine system?"

"Basically, it's a body system you want to work well. Just kick and breathe," said Mr. Ronson. "Use the Force, and all that." Some chuckles traveled down the line of students.

Students attacked the bags. The ki-haps got louder and louder and Ben thought they would have frightened an entire army of assassins.

"Now," said Mr. Ronson, "combinations. Jab. Cross. Round kick. 'HI-YAH!'"

When it was Ben's turn, he tightened his core muscles, preparing to attack. He stepped into the jab and twisted his hips into the cross. "HI-YAH!" The bag toppled back and fell.

"Holy smokes," said Mr. Ronson. "Don't make him mad."

Ben grabbed the punching bag and stood it up. He stepped and round kicked it. "HI-YAH!" He toppled the bag again. He ran back in line, smiling the whole time.

He glanced over at his new jacket with pride. His only regret was that his dad hadn't been there to see him win. His dad never would see him win, not anything — he'd passed away when Ben was only six years old.

Still, Ben hoped against hope that he would have been proud of him. If he won in another tournament maybe, then he'd feel — without a doubt — that he'd made his dad proud. And anyway, then he could start an even newer trend:

a triple jacket. If he could just keep his nerves under control, he was pretty sure he could win a medal at Districts and start that new trend after all.

If he could just control his nerves . . .

CHAPTER 2

STAYING PUT

After class, Ben hopped in the car with his mom. As they usually did after practice, they stopped at the mall for a smoothie.

As they walked in the door, Ben saw a row of display booths running down the center of the hall. He recognized Chief Master Lisa Kleisch, one of the highest-ranking black belts in the nation, in one of the booths advertising her dojang. She'd brought along some students. Each one was dressed in a *dobok*, a traditional tae kwon do uniform. Ben could see the huge banner that hung on her kiosk, dwarfing everything else. It said, "We Make Champions Here — Or Your Money Back."

Ben rolled his eyes. Chief Master Lisa always tried to get more students and she always made big promises about creating champions. The thing was, she *had* created champions out of her students. The tournaments had several different forms to be champion of; Chief Master Lisa's students were often those champions.

Not all the time, though, Ben thought to himself and smiled.

One of the students from the booth tried to hand Ben and his mom a flyer, but Ben shook his head. While he and his mom fended off the student, other students gathered in the center of the mall hallway where there were no kiosks. Ben watched as they did a demonstration: spin kicks and sparring moves. Ben couldn't help but be impressed with their technique. He recognized that precision — had competed against them in tournaments. They were always prepared and very disciplined.

One of Chief Master Lisa's best students, James Lee, walked over to Ben and his mom. Ben knew him only from his success at tournaments. James had won a grand championship for sparring as a sixteen-year-old. Ben and everyone else already knew this, but James handed Ben one of Chief Master Lisa's business cards and said, "You should join us. I won the grand championship for sparring as a sixteen-year-old."

"Thanks," said Ben.

"Seriously, you should join our school," said James. "Mr. Ronson is a goof. He isn't serious about tae kwon do. No one from his studio except you wins anything."

Ben narrowed his eyes. "I like him," he said. "He's a great teacher."

Ben's mom laughed. "Well, he doesn't have that many winning students, honey; you have to admit that. And he does joke around a lot." Ben glared daggers at her, but she just shrugged and gave him a look.

He said, "I like that, though. He's not stiff, like other instructors."

As if on cue, Chief Master Lisa walked up. Looking at James, she said, "Wouldn't it be great if Ben trained with us? Can you imagine having a winner like Ben on a winning team like ours?"

James said, crossing his arms and looking at Ben, "I bet we could win Nationals."

Chief Master Lisa nodded. "We're winning all over the place," she said. "I promise parents their kids will go far and I mean it. It's a guarantee. With you on board, I bet we'd be unstoppable."

Ben felt a little flattered, but not enough. He cleared his throat. "Thank you, but I like it at Mr. Ronson's."

Chief Master Lisa said, "A lot of students have left Mr. Ronson's dojang for ours, Ben. There's a reason for that. I've heard he doesn't take anything very seriously, and it shows. You should think of yourself more and about how far you could go."

Ben's mom asked, "A lot of students have left?"

Chief Master Lisa nodded. "Yesterday," she said as she looked at Ben, "we signed Tanner Hartke."

Ben's heart stopped. His best friend? Defected? He couldn't believe it. He thought Tanner had liked it at Mr. Ronson's as much as Ben did. Worse, he couldn't believe Tanner didn't tell him.

Now he knew why Tanner had been acting so weird the day before. Ben's stomach roiled.

Before he could stew more about it, though, James said, "Ben, if you train with us, can you imagine the level of competition? During practice? During tournaments? Everything. We'll totally up each other's games."

Ben set his jaw. It didn't matter what Tanner did. Ben wanted to stay with Mr. Ronson. Period. He reminded him of his dad — he liked how Mr. Ronson joked around but still got things done. His dad had been the same way. "Thanks for the offer," he said. "But I'm staying where I am."

He bowed to Chief Master Lisa. She shrugged and then bowed back. Ben then bowed to James Lee. He just looked at Ben, his eyes turning mean. Finally, he gave a little bow, but Ben knew he didn't want to. He guessed James Lee didn't like to be told no. But that was too bad. Ben would stick with Mr. Ronson.

During the car ride home, Ben texted Tanner. *I can't believe you quit Mr. Ronson's, dude.*

Right away, a text popped back. *Sorry, man. I was going to tell you. Just had no time.*

Ben put his phone down in frustration. *No time, no way*, he thought. He knew Tanner just hadn't wanted to tell him.

After a few silent minutes, Ben's mom said, "You know, you really should train with them, I think. Mr. Ronson doesn't seem to take things as seriously as the other studio."

Ben stared at his mom. "He's better than Chief Master Lisa. I won Regionals with him."

"Sure, you won Regionals. But Districts is different. It's harder and you're up against older students," she said. "You've seen Chief Master Lisa's students at tournaments. Don't you want a guaranteed win?"

Ben set his jaw. "I have a guaranteed win with Mr. Ronson." After his mom stayed silent for a moment, he tried a different tack. "Anyway, I don't want to train with James Lee. I've heard he can be mean."

His mom looked at him. "He'd kick it up a notch in practice, though," she said. "That's how you get better. Tanner was the only one who pushed you at Mr. Ronson's."

"James Lee would probably kick it up a notch outside of practice, too. And anyway, Mr. Ronson pushes me. He pushes me all the time." Ben felt a pang of sadness. Not having Tanner to train with was a huge disappointment. He always loved going one on one with him.

"Well, Mr. Ronson is supposed to push you as the instructor," his mom said. "At Chief Master Lisa's, you'd have her, James, Tanner, and her entire crew."

Ben was quiet for a minute. Then he said, "Dad would stay at Mr. Ronson's."

His mom's lips tightened. Her shoulders lifted in a huge sigh. "If your father were still alive, he would want you to do what was best for you," she said. "I think you should switch."

A terrible song came on, one that Ben hated. Still, he reached over and turned the volume up louder. His mom took the hint and stopped talking.

When they got home, Ben went straight to the basement, where he'd made a sort of makeshift studio complete with its own punching bag. Ben rolled his neck and started punching it lightly. He needed to work out some of his frustration. After warming up his muscles, he punched the bag as hard as he could. It felt good.

Ben saw his *Ssahng Jeol Bahng* — his nunchucks — in the corner. He grabbed two pairs, one for each hand. He spun them like the blades of a chopper. Hip. Hip. Circle up. Three-sixty. Ben twirled the chains over his wrists and switched handles. He whirled the chain over his shoulder and took the other around his hip. He raised one arm, spun, and came down in a helicopter strike.

He whipped both of the handles down and up in the shape of a V. He repeated. V-strike! V-strike! V-strike!

He did not want to train with Chief Master Lisa. Ben shot his leg up and curved into a crescent kick. He smashed the nunchucks into the punching bag. The wooden handles thudded off the hard rubber. If the punching bag had kneecaps, Ben would have crushed them with the handles of his nunchucks.

His thoughts attacked him. Tanner. James Lee. Chief Master Lisa. They came at him like warriors. Ben whirled the nunchucks. He engaged. The imaginary invaders drove him into a corner. Ben somersaulted between his attackers. He sprung up. With a flurry of side kicks, v-strikes, hook kicks, and up-thrusts, Ben gained some ground.

The thoughts morphed into assassins — three of them, on the attack. One assassin flipped across the floor. Ben stepped back. The assassin unleashed a series of kicks. Ben countered with his nunchucks. He smashed them into the assassin's head. The assassin stumbled backward and disappeared.

Two assassins left to defeat.

One engaged with a sword. Ben dropped the nunchucks and grabbed a sword off the weapons rack. Ben's sword was made of hard plastic and endorsed by the National Tae Kwon Do Association for tournament competition. Ben blocked a strike to his head. He drove his sword into the assassin's side. The assassin doubled over and disappeared.

One left. This assassin threw his sword to the ground. He dropped his throwing stars and stepped into a fighting stance.

Ben let his sword fall. He stepped into a fighting stance, too.

The assassin side kicked at Ben's head. Ben blocked the kick and countered with a punch. The assassin blocked the punch, slid behind Ben, pushed him forward, and tripped him.

Ben rolled to safety and stood up. The assassin kicked him in the face, in the chest, in the gut. The assassin elbowed him in the head. Ben shoved, and the assassin stumbled back. He inhaled. The assassin drove a knife-hand strike at Ben's neck. He blocked and yelled, "HI-YAH!"

Ben punched the assassin in the stomach, and the assassin disappeared.

He caught his breath and glanced at his father's picture. Ben had put the photo on the table in the basement so he could feel like his father was watching him train. Ben always remembered how great he was. He remembered their fun times in the park, swinging and laughing. He always seemed to know what to do.

I'm staying at Mr. Ronson's, he thought. *I don't care if Tanner left. I don't care if my mom thinks I should leave. My decision. I'm staying.*

CHAPTER 3

NO FUN ALLOWED

The next day, Ben's mom took him to observe a class at Chief Master Lisa's studio. Ben hated the idea, but his mom talked him into at least watching a class. Ben thought it might actually help him — maybe he would get some insight about his competition for the tournaments coming up.

When they got there, Ben saw Tanner in his dobok, chatting with some other students. When Tanner saw him, his face lit up and he jogged over. "Dude, you should totally join this place. It's awesome."

Ben shrugged his shoulders. He glared at Tanner. "I like Mr. Ronson's," he said. "I'd never abandon him." Ben made sure to emphasize the word "abandon." He still couldn't believe Tanner hadn't told him he was leaving. And seeing him in the dobok talking with other students made his blood boil.

Tanner looked away. Finally, he said. "I had my reasons," and looked at the crowd of parents standing around chatting. "You should think about joining so we could spar together." Then he jogged back to the other students. Ben felt a pang of anger. Evidently his "reasons" were good enough to leave his best friend.

As he and his mom sat down to watch the class, Ben looked everywhere but at Tanner. The first thing he noticed, though, was that the class did not bow to the parents. Both Ben and his mom had always thought bowing to the parents was a nice gesture. Chief Master Lisa conducted class without any jokes at all. She was so serious Ben wondered if anyone was actually having fun. At Mr. Ronson's, at least people smiled. Ben thought Chief Master Lisa's style seemed super boring, but whenever he looked at his mom, she was nodding or looking on intently. The whole class, especially James Lee, looked so intense Ben wondered if anyone actually liked coming here.

Class finally ended. Chief Master Lisa walked over with Tanner and James and started her sales pitch again. "We got two more people from Ronson's today. Two more soon-to-be champions. Ben, you'll make three." Chief Master Lisa looked at Ben's mom. "Are you ready to sign?"

Ben said, "We have a contract at Mr. Ronson's."

"I can buy it out," said Chief Master Lisa. "That's what I've been doing, when it's worth it.

Ben, with you on the team, I think we can win every single competition at Districts. You would definitely get another championship title. Do you really want to take a chance that you won't win? I can help you with any nerves you might have during a tournament."

Ben's mom said, "We're very interested."

Tanner looked at Ben. "Seriously, Ben. It would be so cool to keep practicing together, right?"

Ben felt conflicted. He'd had a big problem with nerves the last tournament — clearly, since Chief Master Lisa had even mentioned it. He never had a problem with nerves at Mr. Ronson's dojang, so wasn't expecting it in the tournament. Maybe not feeling comfortable at this dojang would actually help. Plus, it would be nice to keep practicing with Tanner. But the intense faces from the practice session kept flashing behind his eyes. No jokes, no fun, all business. He could get great technique and also enjoy his time at Mr. Ronson's.

Maybe he could just ask Mr. Ronson to help him with tamping down his nerves.

He shook his head and said, "See ya later." He gave a little bow to the three in front of him and grabbed his mom to get out of there.

During the drive home, Ben's mom started in on him again.

"I really think you should join, Ben. If you want to win, you have to get serious."

Ben rolled his eyes. "Not that serious, though. They were like zombies in there."

"OK, sure, it's not the same atmosphere at Mr. Ronson's. But did you see how good everyone was? They were super focused."

Ben did the same move as before: he turned up the terrible song on the radio. But this time, Ben's mom turned it down. She said, "Tell me what it is you like better at Mr. Ronson's."

Ben didn't hesitate. "Mr. Ronson."

"Aside from Mr. Ronson."

At this, Ben had to think. "He just . . . the whole dojang makes me feel comfortable. And Mr. Ronson makes sure it's fun." He wasn't sure about adding the next part, but he went for it. "The way he jokes around somehow reminds me of Dad."

His mom squinted at the road and took almost a full minute to say anything. She sighed. "Oh, honey," was all she said.

Ben stayed silent for the rest of the ride. For some reason, he felt embarrassed. Even though he'd told the truth.

At home, Ben went downstairs, down to the home dojang. He palm-heeled the punching bag over and over — it was the noisiest thing he could think of to do. He wanted his mom to know he was not happy. It worked. His mom yelled down the stairs, "Ben, I know you're mad, but can you please keep it down?"

In bed that night, Ben lay awake thinking about why he wanted to stay at Mr. Ronson's.

When Ben had learned the *Choong Jung* form, Mr. Ronson had made up some funny scenarios to help Ben remember the moves.

"The first move," his instructor had said, "is a knife-hand square block, in case someone comes at you with a knife-hand square punch. Mr. Benjamin, have you ever heard of a knife-hand square punch?"

"No, sir."

"That's because there isn't one. Nonetheless, the National Tae Kwon Do Association mandates that the first move of Choong Jung is a knife-hand square block. Make sense?"

"No, sir."

"It's not supposed to."

Ben laughed and then tried to keep his face straight. Mr. Ronson gave him a mock serious look. "Mr. Benjamin, there will be no laughing at nonsense here," which made Ben laugh harder. Mr. Ronson went on.

"Choong Jung also requires a ridge-hand strike," he said. "Take your thumb and index finger and make a ridge. Then, twist your wrist, and smash someone upside the head." Ben and Mr. Ronson practiced their ridge-hands.

Mr. Ronson said, "Have you ever seen a Shakespeare play?"

Ben shook his head.

"A worthy goal for later, Mr. Benjamin. Anyway, in many Shakespeare plays," said Mr. Ronson, "people eavesdrop. They'll hide behind curtains and listen in on other people's conversations. Do this ridge-hand like you're going to give an eavesdropper a good whack. Step up, twist your wrist into the curtain, and slam! Hit that ne'er-do-well right in the ear."

He continued, "You know what else about Shakespeare, Mr. Benjamin? Characters go to great lengths to lie. Characters go to great lengths to see if they've been lied to. With this next move, the horizontal back elbow with a ki-hap, do it like you've discovered someone lying to you. Make sure to yell, 'HI-YAH!'"

Ben leaned into the horizontal back elbow. "HI-YAH!"

Good," said Mr. Ronson. "I don't believe you've been lied to, though, Mr. Benjamin. No need to be so violent." Ben cracked up again.

"For the reverse-hook kick," Mr. Ronson said, "this one's cool. Imagine you're traveling up a quaint path in the wilderness. An assassin darts from behind a tree. You must engage. You spin and . . ." Mr. Ronson spun and reverse-hook kicked powerfully enough to stifle an assassin.

Ben spun and reverse-hook kicked.

"Hmm. I'm afraid you might have died, Mr. Benjamin," said Mr. Ronson. "That assassin might have gotten you. Pity. You had such promise. We'll have to work on it to make sure you don't die quite so easily. Have we ever done an X-block?"

"No sir," said Ben.

"I didn't think so," said Mr. Ronson. "It's extremely practical. Imagine someone attacks you with a bow staff. They're trying to slam that thing down on your head. You need to thrust your arms up across your body, into an X, and then raise it up to block the strike."

"Mr. Ronson, sir," said Ben.

"Yes, Mr. Benjamin."

"Have you ever been attacked with a bow staff, sir?" Ben asked.

"Yes," said Mr. Ronson. "Every single day. I have people trying to brain me with a bow staff constantly. You bet, sir. Every single day."

Ben still laughed to himself about those lessons. He fell asleep smiling at the memories.

Later, he woke up. He'd had a dream that his father was alive and joking with the guys from his army unit, just like they used to in real life. Just like Mr. Ronson did with Ben. Their tales were as far-fetched and adventurous as Mr. Ronson's were. Now, the only place Ben heard talk like that was at Mr. Ronson's studio. He missed the laughter that used to ring through the house.

The thought made him feel alone.

CHAPTER 4

BEST FRIENDS AGAIN

At the Ronson Tae Kwon Do Studio the next day, Ben bowed in and started stretching. Mr. Ronson came out and said, "Mr. Benjamin, how goes the battle?"

Ben took a deep breath and said, "Not good." He needed to let Mr. Ronson know about the past few days.

"Why?" Mr. Ronson asked.

"Chief Master Lisa is stealing your students."

Mr. Ronson looked around the gym and sighed. "Unfortunately this is nothing new. I'd just hoped she'd give it a rest . . . But, that's not our focus here. Back to business. You're dropping your shoulder, Mr. Benjamin. Work on your form."

He turned around and walked into his office. Through the window, Ben saw Mr. Ronson open a ledger on his desk. He sat down and rubbed his hand over his face. Ben worried all through class.

During the car ride home, Ben's mom must have been able to tell that he was upset. She didn't even press him about changing studios. Instead, she said, "Want to get pizza?"

Ben didn't answer. He looked out the window until they got home.

When he got home, though, he felt restless. He bounced around the house, even when he was eating pizza. His mom gave him exasperated looks. Around seven o'clock he sat on the couch, wondering how he could feel better.

His mom said, "Ben, you need to find something to do with yourself or you're going to drive me batty."

Ben shrugged and frowned. But then he sat up straight. Training. That was definitely something to do. Something he *needed* to do. He had to train for Districts. If he could win Districts, besides making his dad proud, maybe he could show all those students how good Mr. Ronson was at his job and they would come back, too. And maybe he could show his mom that he made the right decision to stay with Mr. Ronson.

The only problem was that he and his normal sparring partner weren't talking. He bounced his legs on the edge of the couch.

Finally, he made a decision and yelled to his mom in the kitchen. "Can I throw out the bat signal?"

Ben's mom came out of the kitchen, wiping her hands on a dishtowel. She rolled her eyes. "I suppose. Be back before dark."

He smiled and sprinted to his room to get ready. He took out his phone and wrote a text to Tanner. *Spar at the park?* His finger hovered over the "send" button for a full minute. Finally, he pressed it.

Then he waited a tense two minutes until the text came back: *Sure.* He smiled to himself. They hadn't made up yet, but this was a start.

He grabbed a *Bahng Mahng Ee*, a hard, rubber club resembling a miniature baseball bat, and threw it in his backpack along with some protective sparring pads. Ben went out to the garage and put on his bicycle helmet, then hopped on his bike and pedaled fast to the park.

Ben always loved going to the park, but now, at the beginning of fall with the leaves just starting to turn, he loved it best. He felt thrilled that Tanner was coming: he had really missed him. He needed his sparring partner — even if he had abandoned him for another dojang.

When he got there, Tanner was already sitting on a picnic table near some swings. Ben parked his bike and walked over. He stood for a second, shifting on his feet.

Finally, he sat down beside him and said, "How's Chief Master Lisa's?"

"I hate it," Tanner said.

Ben sat back in surprise. "Why did you sign up then?" he asked.

Tanner looked at him. "My parents made me. They thought I'd get a better education from Chief Master Lisa. And, you know, she promises champions. I didn't want to tell you because I knew you'd be disappointed."

Ben frowned and asked, "So you were lying when you said it was awesome?" Even though Tanner had lied, Ben felt a surge of relief. Maybe the studio wasn't so awesome after all, even with all of Chief Master Lisa's big promises.

Tanner nodded. "Yeah. I miss how Mr. Ronson's studio is actually fun. But I thought if I could get you to switch, it wouldn't be so bad."

Ben took a deep breath. "Yeah, I get that. My mom wants me to switch, too. But I made a commitment to Mr. Ronson. And I think I can get to Districts with him, if I can get past my nerves. I've made up my mind about staying."

Tanner stood up. "I knew you would. But just to warn you: James Lee is gunning for you. And that kid is super intense. He keeps bad-mouthing you. I stand up for you as much as I can, but he's totally going after you at the tournament." He reached into his bag and got out his fighting gear. "So we better get you prepared."

Ben nodded and grabbed his sparring gear. After they suited up and warmed their muscles, Ben and Tanner bowed to each other and started sparring. Ben had forgotten how fun it could be. He started really getting into it, even knocking Tanner in the head.

Tanner said, "Geez. You must still really be mad at me!"

Ben laughed. "Nope! Just getting better at Mr. Ronson's."

Tanner grinned. "Don't rub it in."

They grabbed their Bahn Mahng Ee weapons and bowed and began again. Tanner attacked harder. He thrust his Bahng Mahng Ee at Ben's chest, but Ben blocked it. Tanner twirled his wrist, bringing the club swinging toward Ben's head. Ben ducked and tried to strike Tanner's legs, but Tanner jumped and pounded him in the head. In a tournament, contact to the head while jumping earned contestants three points. Tanner led Ben now 3–2.

Both breathing heavily, they took a second to regroup and then bowed again. This time, Ben went directly for Tanner's head but Tanner was quick enough with his weapon to stop the blow. Ben twirled his wrist for another strike, but Tanner stepped out of the way. He tried to hit Ben in the legs but Ben blocked the blow and stepped back to avoid a counter strike. Except he didn't step quickly enough. Tanner bopped him in the chest for one point. Now Tanner led 4–2.

They caught their breaths. Tanner made a T with his hands for a time out.

Ben took off his helmet and said, "Well, you've definitely gotten better. But when I went to the class, it looked like everyone at Chief Master Lisa's was a zombie."

"They are," said Tanner. "They could be in a zombie tae kwon do movie."

"It seemed like it." Ben looked down and twirled a piece of grass in his hands. "But can they master their endocrine systems?" He looked up at Tanner and smiled.

Tanner laughed. "I still don't know what that means."

"We'll probably never know. But I think he says it to be funny," Ben said.

Tanner grinned. "He does like to joke."

Ben collapsed on the grass and Tanner followed a second later. "So James Lee is really gunning for me?"

Tanner nodded. "Yeah, man. You're the one to beat. And James Lee loves to do the beating. He's really intense. Like, no-one-wants-to-spar-with-him intense. He's going to be tough to beat. Plus he's older. And I think Chief Master Lisa is really pushing him to show you that you're making a mistake."

Ben sighed. "She's not the only one who thinks I am. I guess I'd better keep practicing, huh? I have a lot of people to prove wrong." He stood up.

Tanner stood up, too. "Yeah, dude. We better keep sparring."

Ben said, "That's right. I have to beat *you* first!"

Later that night Ben thought back to the match, which had ended with him on top, 10–8. He'd barely beaten Tanner. And as good as Tanner was, James Lee was much better. Ben knew he had far to go to get his level up. With only three weeks left until Regionals — and then Districts not too long after that — it was time to get serious.

CHAPTER 5

REGIONALS

With so little time to go, Ben wanted to work on as much as he could at the studio. He worked with Mr. Ronson to perfect his Ssahng Jeol Bahng form. Mr. Ronson attacked and Ben fought off the blows using move after move, ducking, weaving, and blocking.

Next, Mr. Ronson bowed to Ben and they worked with the Bahng Mahng Ee. Mr. Ronson was an animal with the Bahng Mahng Ee. He faked to Ben's chest and whacked him in the head almost every time. Ben had to concentrate hard to keep up. By the end of the practice, he was covered in sweat but smiling. There were at least two times when Ben had ducked and turned and avoided Mr. Ronson's attack. He felt pretty proud of that.

He asked him what to do about nerves when the time came, but all Mr. Ronson said was, "That's something you'll have to figure out for yourself."

Ben couldn't help but feel disappointed.

Leading up to the regional tournament, Ben also practiced with Tanner, sparring in the park until they were both out of breath. Before, it took him an entire match to beat Tanner. But Ben knew things were getting better when he won their last bout 10–5. Tanner had clapped him on the back. "Well, maybe James Lee won't kill you after all!" he'd said.

Ben snorted. "Gee, thanks."

But Tanner had just grinned and the two rode their bikes back home.

Finally, the regional tournament came. The night before, Ben woke up with his heart pounding. He'd had a bad dream involving James Lee, a nunchuck, and his father. He lay in bed and turned on the light, then picked up the picture of his dad that he kept on his nightstand.

Sometimes he missed his dad so much it physically hurt. More than anything, he just wanted to make him proud. He wondered if his dad really would have stayed with Mr. Ronson. He wondered if all his practice would be good enough.

Ben rolled around for hours, always coming back to the picture of his dad. The National Tae Kwon Do Association's Regional Tournament meant something. It meant win or go home. Only the first and second place winners in each event could continue to the District Championship. Ben desperately wanted to be in that first place spot.

Finally, Ben found some restless sleep. When he woke up the next morning, though, it felt like he hadn't slept at all.

At the high school where the tournament took place, Ben and his mom walked in and searched for Mr. Ronson. Ben groaned when he saw James and Chief Master Lisa inside the door with a handful of business cards.

Chief Master Lisa saw him and said, "Talk to Tanner Hartke about our gym. He loves it."

Ben smiled. He had talked to Tanner Hartke. He'd also trained with him, specifically so he could beat Chief Master Lisa's best student. With a small bow, he kept smiling and just turned away.

Twenty athletic mats had been set up in the gym to form sections for competition. Each section had three chairs, one for each judge. The fans had to stand, and a bunch of onlookers had already begun jockeying for position.

Ben found the mat where the Ssahng Jeol Bahng Forms competition would take place. He did some push-ups to warm up. Competitors did cartwheels, round offs, and flips. Ben joined them in their aerial acrobatics. Finally, Mr. Ronson arrived.

"Mr. Benjamin!" he said. "Those flips look a little shaky. Are you all right?"

"I'm nervous," Ben said.

"Nerves are good beforehand," said Mr. Ronson as he clapped him on the back. "But even better is when you learn to control them."

Ben thought to himself, *Thanks for the great advice*. He swallowed down his frustration.

The announcer spoke over the loudspeaker, and it was time to go. Mr. Ronson smiled at Ben. Ben tried to smile back.

The judges bowed in and began the contest. After what seemed like ages, Ben's name was called. He took a stand on the mat and bowed in with his Ssahng Jeol Bahng at his side. When he heard the word *seijak*, the Korean word for "begin," he began with a series of v-strikes to get the weapon moving.

He took a deep breath to calm himself, then maneuvered into a series of low blocks and outer blocks. The sticks of his Ssahng Jeol Bahng whirled. He spun to do a side kick. Jump-front-kick. Ben felt his nervousness disappearing a little bit. He took a few quick steps and executed an aerial. His nunchucks sliced through the air.

Stop. Back elbow. Punch, punch. Ben leaned into a back handstand and flipped over to the corner of the mat. He fired up his Ssahnh Jeol Bahng. Ben yelled "HI-YAH!" and did an aerial in the middle, unleashing a series of side kicks, round kicks, and crescent kicks.

He rolled into a somersault, sprang up on one knee, and jabbed with his weapon. Ben finished with a half dozen jumping and spinning crescent kicks and a loud ki-hap. He brought the sticks to a stop. He moved the weapon to his side.

The crowd applauded loudly, but Ben's mom and Mr. Ronson clapped the loudest. Ben felt great. He was pretty sure he'd nailed this one.

The judge in charge of hand technique gave him a 9.8 out of 10. The judge in charge of foot technique gave him a 9.8. The judge in charge of the overall form gave him a 9.7.

Hearing the scores, Ben frowned. He'd hoped for a 9.9 from each of the judges. Maybe his nerves had messed him up more than he thought.

Mr. Ronson and Ben's mom both fist-bumped Ben as he walked off the mat. Mr. Ronson said, "Mr. Benjamin, nice job. You're in first place."

But Ben shook his head. "Doesn't matter. It won't be enough," he said, as he put his equipment in the bag. James Lee had yet to compete, and then Ben would for sure lose his first place standing.

He tried to swallow down his disappointment and think about what was coming up.

When it was James's turn, he caught Ben's eye and shot him a mean smile and mouthed the word "loser." The move surprised Ben — evidently James wouldn't even pretend to have sportsmanship.

James began his form as if he were fighting for his life. Ben thought the routine was cheesy. James ki-happed after almost every move. There were too many jumps, too many spins, and too many rolls. The whole thing looked like James was all show and no substance.

But the judges seemed to love it. Every one of them gave James a 9.9. James took first and Ben took second in that form.

After the first and second places were announced, James walked by Ben. He whispered, "Get used to being a loser, Bennie. Stay at your loser dojang and this is your life." Before Ben could say anything, James walked off. Ben joined Mr. Ronson and his mom, furious about his encounter with James.

Mr. Ronson told Ben, "You can get him in Bahng Mahng Ee sparring." Ben knew Mr. Ronson meant well, but still . . . Ben just hadn't performed as well as he needed to. He tried to get his nerves under control and concentrate on the next contest.

CHAPTER 6

NERVES ARE BACK

Ben couldn't wait for the Bahng Mahng Ee Sparring competition. He definitely felt like bonging some people in the head with a hard-rubber club. The tournament wasn't over yet. He put on his sparring pads. He still had a chance. If he could just beat James at sparring . . .

The loudspeaker crackled overhead with the announcement of the sparring competition. Ben barely had a chance to think before the matches started. But start they did and Ben attacked opponents in the head, body, and legs, and racked up points. He won match after match. When the time came to spar with James, Ben was tired but ready. Still, nerves made him sweat just a little bit more. He hoped he could keep them under control.

James and Ben bowed to each other. James smirked at him. Ben rolled his eyes at the same time a trickle of sweat traveled down his back. He swallowed. The official said, "seijak," and the match began. Ben jumped and smashed James in the head with his Bahng Mahng Ee. Three points for Ben.

The contestants bowed and the action began again. Ben faked a blow to James's body. He flicked his wrist and thwacked the Bahng Mahng Ee onto James's head. Two points! Ben led 5–0. Five more points to go until he could call the match his.

After the next start, Ben faked a lunge at James's chest and then attacked his legs. One point! Ben led 6–0.

The next bow ended and James yelled "HI-YAH!" as he tried to hit Ben's torso. Ben blocked and countered. James blocked the blow. He jumped and hit Ben in the head, earning three points. Now the score was 6–3.

Next, Ben went for James's leg. James jumped and got Ben in the head. Ben tried to harness his frustration. His lead was gone and his nerves were back. It was now 6–6.

Ben could see James's eyes through the face protector on his helmet. His eyes were total focus, his gaze like a laser beam. Tanner was right — James was intense. Ben looked away. For the next attack, he went for James's head. James blocked the attack, jumped, and whacked Ben in the head. Three points. James now led 9–6.

Ben felt the sweat in his eyes and on his palms. He was furious. How did he let this match get out of control? The official called for action and the two bowed again. Ben knew he had to stop James from scoring. His hands shook and he blinked to get the sweat out of his eyes.

The action began and James did a fake out, acting like he would go for Ben's head. Instead, he hit Ben in the leg. And just like that, the match was over.

James won 10–6.

Ben's mom and Mr. Ronson clapped as Ben walked off the mat. Ben could feel the disappointment dripping off of him. He didn't look his mom or Mr. Ronson in the eye. The word "loser" echoed in his head.

As Ben took off his sparring pads, Mr. Ronson told him, "Get him at Districts, Mr. Benjamin. Get him at Districts." He squeezed Ben's shoulder.

Second place might as well have been last. Ben shook his head. His dumb nerves had gotten in the way again.

He watched as Chief Master Lisa gave one of her students some advice. For the first time ever,

Ben wondered if maybe he should train at her studio after all. He definitely needed to up his game. Competing against James everyday could get him to the next level. It would be terrible, but it actually might be good for him.

He shook his head and looked over at Mr. Ronson and felt a pang of guilt. Nope. He couldn't do that. He'd just have to work harder.

And besides, if he couldn't beat James at Districts, he might have to leave Mr. Ronson's studio anyway. Because it would definitely shut down if all the students went to Chief Master Lisa's.

Ben slammed his sparring helmet into his bag, determined now more than ever to beat James at Districts.

CHAPTER 7

FINDING THE PATH

A few days later, Ben rolled around in his bed and checked the clock. It was 6:30 in the morning. Even though it was crazy early, he decided to call Tanner. He didn't answer, so Ben left a message. Ben threw his sparring gear in his backpack, left his mother a quick note, and went out to the garage. He strapped on his helmet and hopped on his bike.

The sun came up and Ben tore into the dawn, off toward the park.

Tanner arrived, yawning. He said, "This is a little early in the morning, dude."

Ben climbed down from the monkey bars. "It's never too early," he said and grinned.

As they strapped on their gear, Ben had a thought. He loved being in the park and the freedom it gave him. He also seemed to do his best fighting here, when he was relaxed and having fun. He said to Tanner, "Let's do a free-form spar. No out of bounds. No stopping after each point. We can climb on the playground equipment."

"Sounds cool," Tanner said. "Will this help get you past James at Districts? I mean, there's no playground equipment at tournaments."

Ben thought about that. "Yeah, but I think my problem has to do with nerves. I get so nervous at those tournaments and tense up. Out here it's just fun — even more fun than at Mr. Ronson's. Maybe if I can harness that . . . I can beat James."

Tanner shrugged. "That sounds good."

Ben grinned. "I mean, it definitely won't hurt!"

They bowed to each other. Ben ran up the bike ramp. He balanced on the edge and twirled his Bahng Mahng Ee. Tanner stood below and attacked Ben's legs. Ben jumped and regained his balance on the ramp. He struck at Tanner's head. Tanner blocked the blow and again went for Ben's legs. Ben blocked the strike and hit Tanner in the head with his club.

Tanner climbed up on the ramp. Ben somersaulted down. Tanner chased him.

They ran to the swings. Ben leapt. He landed with his foot on the seat of the swing and snagged the chain with his free hand. Ben thrust his weapon at Tanner.

Tanner blocked the attack and leapt onto the next swing. They clubbed at each other while balancing on the swings.

The battle spilled onto a play structure that had a bunch of slides and wooden bridges. Ben and Tanner fought like two swordsmen on a pirate ship, both smiling the entire time.

On the basketball court, Ben and Tanner clubbed each other in the head, chest, and legs. Neither relented.

Finally, the guys bowed and sprawled out exhausted in the grass. They took off their helmets. Ben gave Tanner a fist bump. Ben couldn't stop laughing. Everything about that was fun.

"Dude," Tanner said. "That was awesome!"

"So awesome," Ben said. Then he added, "And no nerves in sight. Free-form sparring might just be my path to victory."

For the first time, Ben thought he might actually be able to beat James. If he could just keep this feeling, he might stand a chance.

CHAPTER 8

A FIGHT IN THE PARK

At the Ronson Tae Kwon Do Studio, Ben
twirled his nunchucks. Mr. Ronson came at him
with a side kick. Ben countered with a move from
his Ssahng Jeol Bahng form. He back flipped out
of the way and went into a series of v-strikes,
yelling, "HI-YAH!"

"Nice moves, Mr. Benjamin. You seem extra
bouncy today," Mr. Ronson said. "Did you win the
lottery last night?"

Ben put his nunchucks down and grabbed a towel. "Kind of," he said, smiling. "I figured out that when I do free-form in the park with Tanner, I forget all about nerves. I think I'm getting better."

Mr. Ronson smiled. Then he clapped his hands together. "Well, then, let's do free-form! I knew you'd figure it out."

Ben grinned. "Knew I'd figure out what?"

Mr. Ronson said, "How to tame those nerves of yours. Something I've learned in my many, many, many years of coaching, Mr. Benjamin. The student finds a way. And that way is always better than what a coach might inflict upon him. So, let's get you practicing!"

Ben shook his head. "So you weren't just trying to get out of coaching me?"

Mr. Ronson smiled and chuckled. "Nope. I put my trust in you. And it paid off."

Ben smiled. Pride blossomed in his chest. Then he said, "You don't think doing free-form will make it hard for me when the tournament comes around? I'm a little afraid of that."

"Well, why do you think you like free-form so much?"

"No pressure, maybe? It also . . ." Ben looked down at his feet. He felt silly saying the next part.

"Don't be shy Mr. Benjamin. I won't bite," said Mr. Ronson.

"Well, it reminds me of playing in the park with my dad. Just fun, you know?" Ben shifted. He half-expected Mr. Ronson to laugh at him. But he looked serious for once.

"That makes perfect sense, Mr. Benjamin. Good memories make for good practice. Good for the endocrine system, too." He winked at Ben. "But we're missing someone, don't you think?"

Ben furrowed his eyebrows. Mr. Ronson said, "Tanner. You need your buddy, right?"

Joy sparked through Ben. Not for the first time that day, Ben understood just how good a coach

Mr. Ronson was. So good he would invite a guy who ditched his gym to make sure Ben got the training he needed.

"All right, let's meet at the park!" Mr. Ronson clapped Ben on the back. "Don't you have a friend to text?"

* * *

Ben ran up the bike ramp and balanced at the top like he'd done the day before. Tanner charged up the ramp. They attacked each other with their Bahng Mahng Ees. Ben executed a roll back down the ramp.

Ben ran into Mr. Ronson when he got up from his roll. He grabbed his nunchucks from the side of the ramp to match Mr. Ronson's. They both twirled their weapons.

"Mr. Benjamin," said Mr. Ronson. "Twirl faster. Match my speed. Match my power."

Ben sped up and delivered more power. Mr. Ronson then said, "Now, even faster, even more powerful. Feel it! Let your body do the work. Don't overthink it."

He did a quick turn away from Mr. Ronson's nunchucks and managed to brush his sleeve.

"Good! Keep it up."

Before Ben could catch his breath, Tanner appeared before him. "Not done yet, guy. Not if you want to beat James!"

Ben and Tanner grabbed their Bahng Mahng Ees again. Their battle spilled over to the park's basketball court. Tanner went after Ben's head. He ducked and struck at Tanner's legs. Tanner jumped and brought his club down at Ben's head again. He blocked the strike and smacked Tanner in the chest but lost his balance. He suddenly felt the pressure of everything again. So he backed up on the court and sat on his knees.

"Dude, what are you doing?" Tanner asked.

Ben heard Mr. Ronson say, "Well, go get him, Tanner. There was no time called."

Ben smiled to himself. No distractions, no nerves — just him and his environment. He listened to his heart beating and thought of his dad. Mr. Ronson was right: he could figure this out himself. If he just felt the stillness inside from being at ease in the park, he could stay calm. When he heard a rustling near him, he jumped up and twirled around just in time to smack Tanner in the head.

"And time!" said Mr. Ronson. He was beaming. "Well done, Mr. Benjamin, well done. You even almost got me. I think you have found your rhythm, sir. Just keep these things in mind at the tournament and you will be unstoppable." He swung his nunchucks. "OK, a quick exercise to get your head on straight. Swing your nunchucks like this, then we drop and do push-ups."

Ben, Tanner, and Mr. Ronson twirled their nunchucks. Mr. Ronson said, "Drop." They all dropped down and did five push-ups. Then they sprang up and swung their nunchucks. Ben loved the sound they made every time they swung around. Mr. Ronson said, "Drop." They dropped down and did five more push-ups.

After three more times, Ben was out of breath and sore, but he felt alive and happy. He thought about his dad and the fun times they'd had in this park. If he could keep this feeling, he might have a chance at Districts. He high-fived Tanner and Mr. Ronson and together they walked out of the park as the sun set behind them.

CHAPTER 9

DISTRICTS

After four long days and three hard workouts, the time had finally arrived.

Districts.

Ben felt the familiar nerves radiate through him. He couldn't seem to shake them and get the carefree, fun feeling from his free-form training, even after all the practices that week. When he began his forms, he knew he was in trouble.

Two forms later, Ben walked away in the exact same spot as the regional tournament — James first, Ben second. Still, he wasn't done yet. He had one more chance: Bahng Mahng Ee Sparring. If Ben could win that event, then he could be a District Champion. He could help Mr. Ronson get some students back. If he couldn't win it, he'd be letting everyone down. Especially himself. Especially his dad.

Mr. Ronson saw the expression on his face. He asked him, "What do you need to do? What will help?"

Ben thought for a second. "I feel like being alone," he said. "I think I need to find that calmness again. Somehow." He frowned, hoping he could get back the feeling from the park again.

"You bet," Mr. Ronson said.

Ben took his bag of sparring gear and walked off. He maneuvered through all the people in the civic center.

Far down the hall, he found a conference room no one was using. He went inside.

The doubt in Ben's mind overwhelmed him. His hands had started shaking again. He was disappointed in himself.

He reached into his sparring bag and pulled out a picture of his father. He held it to his chest and breathed deeply. He wanted more than anything to win so that it would make him proud.

Ben felt warmth spread through him, like someone was giving him a big hug. Excitement started to replace the doubt. A new confidence replaced the nervousness; he could feel it spreading throughout his body. He took a breath and yelled, "HI-YAH!" It echoed through the room. Ben smiled at his own voice. It sounded powerful. It sounded like he could win.

Ben put on his sparring pads. He took his Bahng Mahng Ee out of the bag. He placed the picture of his father on the floor. He whirled his weapon, loving the feel of his muscles as he performed the familiar moves. Then, he dropped for five push-ups. After each push-up, he touched his forehead to the picture of his father.

When he was done, panting slightly, he took one last look at the picture. Suddenly, he knew something he didn't know before as sure as his own heartbeat: His dad was proud of him. Proud of him for sticking to his studio. Proud of him for working hard and not giving up. Proud about this tournament — no matter what. Just proud.

Ben felt the nervous tension drain out of him. He was ready.

CHAPTER 10

MAKING DAD PROUD

When the Bahng Mahng Ee Sparring competition began, Ben felt like he knew what was coming before it even came. A strike to the head? Ben blocked it. A strike to the chest? Ben blocked it. A strike to the legs? Forget it. Ben blocked it.

Ben won his entire bracket. He watched James win the final match of the other bracket. When the official declared James the winner, James pointed at Ben and mouthed the word "Loser."

But Ben wasn't falling for any more intimidation moves, especially one as dumb as James's.

Finally, it was time for the showdown between Ben and James. Ben could feel the adrenaline run through him, giving him focus. Unlike before in tournaments, his nerves seemed to be nowhere in sight. The official called for James and Ben to bow to each other, then said, "seijak." The match began.

They circled and slapped at each other with their clubs. James faked to Ben's chest and tried to hit him in the head. Ben ducked and tagged James's leg for one point. Ben led 1–0.

The official called for action. This time, James went on the offensive. He ran at Ben and swiped at his head. Ben blocked the attack, but James spun and hit Ben anyway. Two points. James led 2–1.

The official called the fighters into action again. Ben thought about his free-form runs with

Tanner and Mr. Ronson. He took a deep breath and remembered how much fun he'd had at the park and how relaxed he'd felt. He faked a blow to James's body. He flicked his wrist and thwacked the Bahng Mahng Ee at James's head. James blocked the strike.

They circled each other again, Ben still breathing evenly. James threw some strikes that Ben blocked. Ben did a back flip into the corner of the mat and sat there with his back to James. James rushed at him. Ben listened for the rustle of his dobok, just as he'd listened for Tanner's footsteps in the park.

When the footsteps came close, Ben swooped around and hit James in the leg, but James had already started a strike to Ben's head. Since Ben's Bahng Mahng Ee made contact first, Ben got the point, but James still clobbered Ben in the head, making his eyes water. He shook it off. The score was tied 2–2.

The contestants bowed, and the action began again. Ben could see James's hard glare from beneath the face protector on his helmet. He rushed at Ben, rearing back with his club and smashing Ben's weapon out of his hands. The rules said that if a fighter dropped his weapon, the opponent received a point. James now led 3–2.

Ben dropped down and did five push-ups. Then, he took a deep breath and readied himself for action. He remembered the picture of his father. He remembered that his dad would be proud no matter what.

The judge called for action again and James rushed at Ben once more. James's Bahng Mahng Ee came soaring toward Ben's head. Ben spun out of the way, jumped up, and smashed James in the head. Three points for Ben. Now Ben led 5–3.

Ben dropped down and did five push-ups again. They bowed. James yelled, "HI-YAH!" Ben thought he could see James harden his glare.

Just like before, he rushed at Ben. He faked a blow to Ben's head and dropped down for Ben's legs. Ben jumped over James's club and walloped James in the head. Three more points. Ben now led 8–3.

James flexed his muscles and growled. He looked at Ben but now Ben saw something new: uncertainty.

Ben dropped and did five push-ups. The judge called for action again. James rushed at Ben and lashed out at his legs. Ben jumped, and tried for James's head, but James blocked the attack. James jumped up and hit Ben in the head.

Ben still led 8–6.

He did five push-ups and then sprang up. He knew it was now or never. Ben thought about his dad and Mr. Ronson. He thought about Tanner and his mom and all the training he'd done. And he thought about how he'd made the absolute right decision to stay with Mr. Ronson. He thought about how his dad was proud. He smiled to himself.

The official called for action. Again, James rushed at Ben. Ben somersaulted behind him and leapt to his feet, as he'd done countless times in the park. James spun around. As soon as James's head was turned, Ben took his Bahng Mahng Ee and clobbered James in the head.

Ben won the match 10–6.

For a minute, it didn't sink in. Then, it hit him: He had placed first in Bahng Mahng Ee Sparring! He was a National Tae Kwon Do Association District Champion. The moment did not seem real.

James fell to his knees and punched the mat. Chief Master Lisa stood on the side with her hands on her hips. She looked disappointed.

Slowly, as the reality of the moment set in, Ben could hear the crowd applauding. His mom, Tanner, and Mr. Ronson were the loudest. This time, Ben was not embarrassed. He walked off the mat and welcomed their congratulations.

Exhausted, he still could not stop smiling. Mr. Ronson said, "You did it! You did it, Mr. Benjamin. I knew you could!"

The crowd kept applauding.

Ben, his mom, Tanner, and Mr. Ronson all hugged each other. Ben's sweaty hair left damp marks on their shirts, but none of them cared.

CHAPTER 11

A NEW TREND

At the Ronson Tae Kwon Do Studio, Ben stretched out beside Tanner. Some new students sat down and joined them.

Ben asked, "Do you know how to master your endocrine system?" Tanner laughed. The new students looked confused. One said, "No."

"You'll have to ask Mr. Ronson," Ben said. "He'd love to explain it."

Mr. Ronson came out of the office. He said, "Welcome to the circus, gentlemen. Everyone here is perfectly normal." He laughed at his own joke as he moved to the front and center of the gym to begin class.

After the students and teacher bowed to each other, Mr. Ronson said, "As a sign of respect turn and bow to the parents." The parents in the sitting area stood up. The students turned and bowed to them. The parents bowed in return.

Mr. Ronson paced in front of a full class. More and more students had been joining, many of them returning from Chief Master Lisa's. Ben's win had shown that there was more than one way to a championship.

Mr. Ronson said, "Ladies and gentlemen, it's time for a magic trick. I'm going to make a championship jacket appear." He reached down behind a speaker and pulled out a championship jacket.

On the back it said, *National Tae Kwon Do Association District Champion Benjamin Davis*.

"Mr. Benjamin, sir," said Mr. Ronson, "they shipped this one a little faster than the other one. I guess we're important now." He held up the jacket for people to admire. "Mr. Benjamin won Districts in the fifteen-, sixteen-, and seventeen-year-old division. He's only fifteen."

Both students and parents applauded.

"If you work hard," said Mr. Ronson, "you can be as awesome as Mr. Benjamin. Mr. Benjamin, sir, please step forward."

Ben stepped up and claimed the jacket. He bowed to Mr. Ronson. As a sign of special appreciation, Ben also bowed to Tanner.

Mr. Ronson said, "What's your goal now? All the way to Nationals?"

"All the way to Nationals, sir," said Ben.

"Well," said Mr. Ronson, "we'd better get to work."

He ki-happed, and the students lined up at the punching bags.

Ben grinned. Somehow he knew without a doubt that his father was proud of him. He imagined his dad giving him a hug and a warm feeling spread all the way through him.

And now he couldn't wait to start the triple jacket trend.

Derek Tellier's work has appeared in *Secret Laboratory*, *New Verse News*, *Ascent Aspirations*, Pindeldyboz.com, and other publications. He holds a Master of Fine Arts degree in Creative Writing from Minnesota State University, Mankato. He is a writer, teacher, and musician in the Twin Cities.

GLOSSARY

aerial acrobatics (AYR-ee-uhl AK-ruh-bat-iks) — gymnastic moves that take place in the air, such as flips, cartwheels with no hands, and so on.

Districts (DIS-trikts)—the last tournament to win before moving on to State championships, and then National championships

endocrine system (END-o-krin SIS-tuhm)—a network of glands that controls certain hormones, affecting the entire body

free-form (FREE-form)—not having a formal shape or pattern

nunchucks (NUHN-chuhks)—a pair of sticks or batons joined by a chain used in some martial arts

Regionals (REE-juhn-uhls)—the last tournament to win before moving on to District championships

sparring (SPAHR-ing)—a type of training that includes practice blows and contact

TAE KWON DO TERMS

If you're new to tae kwon do or need a refresher on some of the terms, here's a great start.

Bahng Mahng Ee—a medium length stick used in combat-weapons sparring

cha ryuht—"attention" in the Korean language

choon bi—"ready" in the Korean language

Choong Jung—a form in tae kwon do

crescent kick—a front kick that starts from the ground and makes a large arc

dobok—the traditional tae kwon do uniform

dojang—the name of the training studio in tae kwon do

hook kick—a side kick that uses a hook motion to catch an opponent with the heel

ki-hap—a loud yell

knife-hand square block—a block using both arms and hands, in the shape of a square, with hands in knife-hand position

knife-hand strike—a strike where the fingers of the hand are extended and the thumb is close to the palm. The outside of the hand is used for the strike.

palm-heel strike—a strike where the fingers of the hand are bent slightly inward, and the fighter uses the palm of the hand to strike

reverse-hook kick—a back kick that uses a hook motion to catch an opponent with the heel. When the kick is complete, the fighter is facing forward.

ridge-hand strike—a strike where the fingers of the hand are extended and the thumb is tucked in. The inside of the hand is used for the strike.

round kick—a kick where the fighter uses his or her back leg to kick frontward

seijak—"begin" in the Korean language

spin kick—a hook kick performed by spinning the body around

X-block—a block where the fighter crosses his or her arms at the forearms and makes an "X"

DISCUSSION QUESTIONS

1. Ben decides to stay at the Ronson Tae Kwon Do Studio even though he is pressured to switch to Chief Master Lisa's. Why did he stay? Would you have stayed?

2. Nerves made it hard for Ben to perform in tournaments. Can you name a time when you were nervous about some type of performance? How did you get over your nerves?

3. Having fun while practicing was important to Ben. Why do you think that is? Do you agree with him that fun can help a practice?

WRITING PROMPTS

1. Ben's father passed away when he was just six years old. Write a letter pretending to be Ben's dad. What do you think he would want to say to Ben about tae kwon do?

2. Tanner had a hard time telling Ben that he had switched to Chief Master Lisa's dojang. Write about a time a friend let you down and about how you made up, if you did.

3. Free-form practice helped Ben calm down and relax. Write down four different activities that help you calm down or just enjoy what you're doing without feeling pressure.

MORE ABOUT
TAE KWON DO

The World Taekwondo Federation is one of the governing bodies of tae kwon do. It is located in Seoul, South Korea.

Tae kwon do (often) has six belt colors. In order of difficulty they are: white, yellow, green, blue, red, and black. The belts get darker as the practitioner gains more experience and skill.

South Korea's military practices tae kwon do as part of its training.

Some say that General Choi-Hong Hi was the founder of modern day tae kwon do, but not everyone agrees.

Tae kwon do is one of two martial arts in the Olympics. (The other one is Judo.)

The English translation of tae kwon do is "way of foot and fist."

The origins of tae kwon do date back to more than 2,000 years ago in Korea.